HENRY GOES VISITING

Story by Jane Pilgrim, Illustrated by F. Stocks May

BROCKHAMPTON PRESS, LEICESTER

AND THE POTATO PRESS, CHICAGO

Published in 1972 in the United States of America by J. Philip O'Hara Inc,
Chicago and in Great Britain by Brockhampton Press Limited, Leicester
Published simultaneously in Canada by Van Nostrand Reinhold Limited, Scarborough, Ontario
This edition Copyright © Brockhampton Press 1972
Printed in Great Britain by Purnell and Sons Limited

Henry was a large grown-up pig. He was also a strong, silent pig, and he lived at Blackberry Farm. He had his own little house in the yard, and he liked to look over his gate and watch the other animals, and sometimes he would talk to them. But not very often, because Henry was a silent pig. He watched and he listened and he thought, and then one day he did something quite new.

One afternoon in October, when Mr. and Mrs. Smiles
and their children, Joy and Bob, were in the fields
picking up potatoes, Henry lifted the latch of
his gate and walked out across the yard and down
the lane. Mother Hen and Mary watched him go.

Later on, just as it was getting dark, Henry
came back. Mother Hen and Mary were waiting
for him. "Henry, Henry, where have you been?"
they clucked. "I've been to London to visit
the Queen," Henry grunted, and went back into
his little house to look for his tea.

"What rubbish!" fussed Mother Hen. "Of course
he hasn't." And she went clucking across the
yard to tell Walter Duck.

The next afternoon Henry went off again,
and the next, and the next, and the next.
By the end of a week the farmyard was in
a flutter, wondering what it was all about.

Ernest Owl called a meeting to discuss the situation.
Emily the Goat turned up with Little Martha the Lamb.
Mother Hen and Mary, of course, were there, and Walter
Duck. George the Kitten turned up late. He always was
late. Lucy Mouse crept in beside Martha when George was
not looking. Rusty could not come, as he was working
in the fields with Mr. Smiles, and Joe Robin was
away on business.

They met in the yard, and listened carefully while
Ernest talked to them about Henry. Ernest sat on an
old bucket near the farm back door, and while he
was speaking Henry came trotting home again. "Hi,
Henry," hooted Ernest, "tell us where you've been!"
But Henry only grunted, and went into his
little house to look for his tea.

Now, all this time Mr. and Mrs. Smiles and Bob and
Joy did not know about Henry, because every day
that week they had been working hard in the fields
to get all the potatoes brought in before the frosts
came. And Henry was always in his little house
waiting for his tea when they came home in
the evening.

The only two who knew about Henry were Mrs. Squirrel
and her daughter Hazel, because they lived in
the old oak tree down the lane from Blackberry
Farm. And every afternoon they saw Henry trotting
past their tree, and every evening he stopped to
talk to them on his way home.

Now, Henry was a silent pig; but he always stopped
and spoke to Mrs. Squirrel, because Mrs. Squirrel
kept a big store of acorns, and all pigs love
acorns. And every afternoon, on his way home,
Mrs. Squirrel gave Henry a bowl of acorns,
and he told her his news.

It was big news. His sister, Henrietta, had just had her first family—twelve little fat, pink pigs, and every afternoon Henry had trotted down to the farm where she lived to visit them, because he was very fond of his sister Henrietta, and he thought her babies were beautiful.

The day after Ernest Owl's meeting,
while Henry was munching his acorns and talking
to Mrs. Squirrel, Joe Robin joined the party
and heard the news about Henrietta.
So off he flew in a hurry to tell Ernest the secret.

Ernest was most interested. He had met Henrietta
once, but he could not understand why Henry would
not tell them himself. "I know," said Joe. "Henrietta
doesn't want everyone at the farm to go down and see
her babies yet, and Henry agrees that it would be
very awkward for her, because there isn't much room
in her little house now. You ask him yourself."

So Ernest met Henry that evening when he came
home, and asked him about Henrietta. And Henry
said he could tell all the others now, because the
babies were allowed to go out and Henrietta was going
to bring them along herself the next afternoon,
to show them to everybody and to have tea with
Henry in his little house.

And the next afternoon Henrietta arrived with
her family. Mr. and Mrs. Smiles and Joy and Bob came
home early and saw them, too, and then everyone
at Blackberry Farm knew why Henry had
been out visiting.